CARTER HIGH
MYSTERIES

THE SECRET ADMIRER
Mystery

By Eleanor Robins

SADDLEBACK
EDUCATIONAL PUBLISHING

CARTER HIGH
M Y S T E R I E S

EDUCATIONAL PUBLISHING
www.sdlback.com

Copyright ©2006, 2011 by Saddleback Educational Publishing

ISBN-13: 978-1-61651-567-6
ISBN-10: 1-61651-567-8
eBook: 978-1-61247-135-8

Printed in Guangzhou, China
0311/CA21100048

15 14 13 12 11   1 2 3 4 5

Chapter 1

It was Friday. Paige was at school. She was in the lunchroom.

Paige was sitting at a table. Lin and Willow were with her. Willow was in her wheelchair.

All three girls were good friends. And all three lived at Grayson Apartments.

Lin seemed very happy. She said, "I can hardly wait until next Friday."

The Carter High school dance was next Friday night.

A boy had called Lin last night. He'd asked her to the dance.

Paige wished someone would ask her, too. But no one had yet.

Paige didn't want to talk about the dance. But she knew Lin wanted to talk about it.

"What are you going to wear, Lin?" Paige asked.

"I don't know yet. My mom said I can buy a new dress. And I'm going to look for one tomorrow," Lin said.

"I hope you find something you like," Paige said.

"I hope so, too, Paige. I'm sure I will," Lin said.

"I'm sure you will, too," Willow said.

Paige wanted a new dress to wear to the dance. But most of all she wanted a date to the dance. And she didn't have that yet.

"Are you and Emmett going to the dance, Willow?" Lin asked.

Emmett was Willow's boyfriend. He went to Newton High. And he was on the football team.

"No. We aren't going to the dance," Willow said.

That surprised Paige. "Why?" she asked.

"Emmett has to work that night. And he can't go to the dance. But that's okay. His school dance is the next weekend. And we're going to it," Willow said.

"What about you, Paige? Are you going to the dance? I hope you are," Lin said.

"I don't know," Paige said.

"Why, Paige? Don't you want to go?" Lin asked.

"Yes. But no one has asked me yet," Paige said.

"Someone will, Paige. The dance isn't until next week," Willow said.

"I know that someone could still ask me. But I don't think anyone will," Paige said.

Lin and Willow seemed very surprised.

"Why do you think that, Paige?" Willow asked.

Paige said, "I haven't had a date in three weeks. That's why I don't think anyone will ask me to the dance."

"Don't worry, Paige. Someone will ask you," Willow said.

"Yes, Paige. Someone will ask you," Lin said.

Paige thought Willow and Lin spoke too quickly. And she wasn't sure they really thought that someone would ask her to the dance.

Chapter 2

It was the next morning. Paige sat in front of her apartment building. Willow was there, too.

The girls were talking about school. But they weren't talking about the school dance.

Paige didn't want to talk about the dance. And she didn't want to hear about it either.

Paige saw Logan, Drake, and Jack. The three boys lived at Grayson Apartments. They were good friends. And they were good friends with Paige and Willow, too.

The boys came over to talk to Paige and Willow.

Logan said, "I know what you two girls were talking about." Then he laughed.

Paige knew Logan didn't know anything. But she wanted to know what he thought they were talking about anyway.

"What were we talking about?" Paige asked.

"The school dance. What else?" Logan asked.

"Yeah," Drake said.

"That's for sure," Jack said.

Paige said, "You're wrong. We weren't talking about the dance."

"Well we were," Logan said.

"Who are you taking to the dance?" Willow asked.

Drake and Jack quickly told Willow. But Logan didn't say anything.

Willow asked, "What about you, Logan? Who are you taking to the dance?"

"I don't know yet," Logan said.

Logan liked to date many girls. And he never dated one girl for very long.

Willow said, "You should ask someone soon, Logan."

"Yes, Logan. You should ask someone soon," Jack said.

"I still have a lot of time. The dance isn't until next week," Logan said.

"You need to ask someone now, Logan. Girls don't like to be asked at the last minute," Willow said.

"That's right, Logan. I wouldn't want to be asked at the last minute," Paige said.

"Maybe. But you would still go with the guy," Logan said. Then he laughed.

Paige looked at Logan. And she didn't say anything. But she didn't like what

Logan just said.

Willow said, "That wasn't a nice thing to say to Paige, Logan."

"No. That wasn't nice," Paige said.

"I was only joking," Logan said.

But Paige wasn't sure that he was.

"Do you have a date to the school dance, Paige?" Logan asked.

"No," Paige said.

"But you'll have a date, Paige. The dance isn't until next Friday," Willow said.

Logan said, "Let me see if I get this right. I should ask a girl for a date now. But it's okay for some other guy to ask Paige next week."

That made Paige mad.

"Don't worry about me. And don't worry about who I go to the dance with," Paige said.

And she didn't say that in a nice way.

Logan said, "Don't get mad at me, Paige. It isn't my fault you can't get a date to the dance."

That made Paige even more upset. But she was too upset to say anything to Logan.

"That wasn't nice, Logan," Willow said.

"That's for sure," Jack said.

"I'm sorry, Paige. I was only joking. I tell you what I'll do. I'll ask around. And I'll find a date for you," Logan said.

"I can get my own date. I don't need your help," Paige said.

"Don't say anything else, Logan," Willow said.

"Yeah, Logan," Drake said.

"That's for sure," Jack said.

Logan liked to joke. But much of the time Paige didn't think he was funny.

For a few minutes the five didn't talk. But Paige was thinking about the school dance.

The three guys were her friends. So maybe she should tell them why she was so upset.

Paige said, "I haven't had a date in three weeks. And I don't think anyone will ask me to the dance."

The three guys seemed surprised.

At first no one said anything. But then Logan asked, "What about Brett? Some days he talks to you after science class. Maybe he'll ask you."

"Brett just wants to know what my class did in English. We have the same teacher," Paige said.

"I can hint to him that you need a date to the dance. Do you want me to do that?" Logan asked.

That made Paige mad again.

"I can get my own date," Paige said.

And Paige didn't speak to Logan in a nice way.

"Okay. Okay. What about Cullen?" Logan asked.

Cullen was in Paige's art class. Sometimes he sat next to Paige in class.

"Cullen has a girlfriend," Paige said.

And Paige didn't think Cullen wanted to date any other girl.

The guys left to play ball. Willow started to talk about something else. And Paige was glad that she did.

Then Paige didn't have to talk about the dance. And she didn't have to hear about the dance either.

But Paige still thought about the dance. And she still wanted a date. Would anyone ask her to the school dance?

Chapter 3

It was Monday. Paige was at school. She was at her locker.

Paige saw Logan. He stood there talking to Brett.

Logan waved at Paige. Then he hurried down the hall.

Brett walked over to Paige.

Brett asked, "What did your class do in English today?"

"We went over our homework. Then we had a surprise test," Paige said.

"Do you think you did okay on it?" Brett asked.

"Yes. But I did my homework. Some

of the class didn't. So I don't think some people did well on the test," Paige said.

"I did my homework, too. So I should do okay if my class has a test. And I'm sure we'll have one, too," Brett said.

Logan hurried back over to them. He said, "I need to borrow your science book, Paige."

Brett didn't say anything else to Paige. And he walked on down the hall.

"Why do you need my book, Logan? Where's your book?" Paige asked.

"It isn't in my locker. So I guess I left it at home. Hurry and give me your book. I don't want to be late to class," Logan said.

"But I'll need my book this morning," Paige said.

"But you won't need it for the next class. So hurry and let me borrow it. I'll give it back to you in art class," Logan said.

"Okay. But be sure you bring it to class," Paige said.

"I will. Just hurry and give me your book. I can't be late to Mr. Zane's class," Logan said.

Mr. Zane was Logan's science teacher.

"You know how Mr. Zane is. He would make me stay after school for a month," Logan said.

Paige knew Logan was joking about that. Mr. Zane would make him stay after school only one afternoon.

Paige got her science book out of her locker. She made sure no papers were in the book. Then she gave her science book to Logan.

"Thanks," Logan said.

"Don't forget to bring my book to art class," Paige said.

"Don't worry, Paige. I won't forget," Logan said.

Then Logan walked down the hall.

Paige shut her locker. She started to quickly walk down the hall. She was in a hurry. And she almost bumped into Cullen from her art class.

"Hey, watch where you're going, Paige," Cullen said.

"Sorry," Paige said.

Paige thought Cullen was going to say something else to her. But then a guy called to him.

Cullen hurried over to the guy. Then the two guys walked away. And Paige hurried to her next class.

Chapter 4

Later that morning, Paige sat in her art class. Logan wasn't there yet. Paige hoped he didn't forget to bring her book. She needed it for her next class.

Then Logan came in. He had a book in his hand. He hurried over to Paige. He gave the book to her.

"Here's your science book, Paige. Thanks," Logan said.

"I'm glad you brought my book. I thought you might forget to bring it," Paige said.

Paige put the book on her desk.

She saw Cullen come in. He came over

to the desk next to hers. And he sat down.

Then Logan asked, "What were you and Brett talking about this morning?"

"He was asking me about English," Paige said.

Logan said, "Too bad. I thought he might have asked you to the dance."

Paige started to get mad.

"Why did you say that? Did you tell Brett I needed a date to the dance? I told you not to do that," Paige said.

And Paige didn't say that to him in a nice way.

"I didn't. I didn't. Don't get upset," Logan said.

Paige looked over at Cullen. He was looking at them. He might have heard what Logan said. And now he might know she didn't have a date.

The bell rang. It was time for the class to start.

Paige put her science book in her backpack. She didn't look inside the book before she did.

Paige liked her art class. So the class time went by quickly for her.

Soon the end of class bell rang. Then Paige picked up her backpack. She started walking to the door. Logan came over to her.

Logan said, "Don't forget your science book, Paige."

Paige knew Logan was trying to be funny again. She'd said she thought he might forget her book. So he had to tell her not to forget the book.

"I'm not the one who forgets books. You are," Paige said.

Then Paige hurried to her science class. The bell rang to start class.

Paige opened her backpack. She got out her science book.

She knew what page the lesson would start on. So she opened her book. And she started to look for that page.

But then Paige found a piece of paper in the book. The paper was folded in half.

Paige wondered what Logan had left in her book. She hoped he didn't need it before lunch.

Paige unfolded the paper. It was a note to her. And someone had typed it.

```
Dear Paige,

     I want to ask you to the
dance. But I'm not sure you'll
say yes. That's why I haven't
asked you.

          Your Secret Admirer
```

Paige got very mad. She knew Logan had left the note in her book. She knew he wanted her to find it. But why?

Did he do it as a joke? Or did he do it because he felt sorry for her? Did Logan think the note would make her feel better?

Paige didn't know which reason made her more upset.

Now she knew why Logan didn't want her to forget her book. He wanted her to find the note.

Paige could hardly wait until it was time for lunch. She had a lot to say to Logan. And it wasn't about how happy she was with him.

Chapter 5

Paige hurried into the lunchroom. She was still mad at Logan. And she could hardly wait to talk to him.

Paige got her lunch. Then she looked for Logan.

She saw Logan. He was at a table. Lin and Drake were with him.

Paige hurried over to the table.

She put her tray on the table. The tray made a loud noise.

Then Paige sat down at the table.

Logan asked, "What is wrong with you, Paige? You seem mad."

"I'm mad. And you know why," Paige said.

Logan seemed surprised at what Paige just said.

"How would I know?" Logan asked.

Paige asked him, "How could you do that?"

"Do what?" Logan asked.

"You know what," Paige said.

"What did Logan do?" Drake asked.

"Yeah, Paige. What did Logan do?" Lin asked.

"Logan knows I don't have a date to the dance. And he knows I think no one will ask me. So he wrote a note to me. And he put it in my science book," Paige said.

"What did the note say?" Lin asked.

"The note said he wanted to ask me to the dance. But he wasn't sure I would say yes. So that was why he hadn't asked me.

Then he signed it, Your Secret Admirer,"
Paige said.

"Why did you do that?" Drake asked.

"Yes, Logan. Why did you do that?
Did you do it as a joke? Or did you do
it because you feel sorry for me?" Paige
asked.

"I don't know what you're talking
about, Paige. I didn't write a note to you,"
Logan said.

"I know it was you. No one else could
have put it in my science book," Paige
said.

"Let me see the note, Paige. I know
what Logan's handwriting looks like. It's
messy. So I would know it anywhere,"
Drake said.

"Logan was too smart for that. He
didn't want me to know for sure that
he wrote the note. So he typed it," Paige
said.

Logan said, "I don't know what you're talking about, Paige. I didn't write a note to you. I didn't type a note to you. And I didn't put a note in your science book either."

"You really didn't do it?" Lin asked.

"No. I didn't," Logan said.

"Then I believe you," Lin said.

"You aren't playing a joke on Paige, Logan?" Drake asked.

"No. I wouldn't play that kind of joke on Paige," Logan said.

"But it had to be you, Logan. It can't be anyone else," Paige said.

"Why do you think that?"

Paige said, "Logan borrowed my science book. But I made sure it didn't have any papers in it. And the note was in the book when Logan gave it back to me."

"I don't know how the note got in your book, Paige. But I didn't put it in there," Logan said.

"Then who did put the note in the book?" Drake asked.

But no one had an answer for that.

Chapter 6

The four were still at lunch. They ate for a few minutes. But they didn't talk.

Paige knew Logan liked to joke with all of them. But she didn't think he would lie to all of them.

Logan said he didn't put the note in her book. And now she didn't think he did either.

But who else could have put the note in her book?

Paige said, "I have to find out who wrote the note."

"But how will you do that, Paige?" Drake asked.

"I don't know," Paige said.

"We'll help you find out, Paige," Lin said.

"Yeah," Logan said.

"When did you find the note, Paige?" Lin asked.

"When I got to my science class," Paige said.

"Did anyone else have the book?" Lin asked.

Paige said, "No. But I believe Logan. And now I don't think he put the note in my book. But I don't know how anyone else could have."

Drake said, "We could ask around the school. And maybe we could find out who did it."

"No. You can't do that," Paige said.

"Okay. I won't. But why?" Drake asked.

"Because all of Carter High will know I don't have a date. And I don't want everyone to know," Paige said.

"So what do you want us to do, Paige?" Drake asked.

"I don't know," Paige said.

Logan said, "Maybe Cullen put the note in your book. I think he likes you. He looks at you a lot in art class."

"Cullen looks at girls in my class, too," Drake said.

Paige said, "I told you Cullen has a girlfriend, Logan. And I'm sure he didn't put the note in my book."

"How can you be sure?" Drake asked.

Logan said, "Yeah, Paige. How can you be sure? I gave the book to you. And you put it on your desk. You walked around during art class. Cullen could have put the note in your science book then."

"He couldn't have," Paige said.

"But how do you know that, Paige?" Lin asked.

"Yeah, Paige. You didn't look at Cullen during all of class. Or did you?" Logan said.

Logan was joking with her again. And Paige didn't like that.

Lin said, "We don't have time for you to make jokes, Logan. We need to help Paige find out who wrote the note. She might want to go to the school dance with him."

"You said Cullen couldn't have put the note in your book. Why do you think that, Paige?" Drake asked.

Paige said, "I put the book in my backpack. I did that as soon as the bell rang. So Cullen didn't have a chance to put anything in my book."

"Are you sure?" Lin asked.

"Yes," Paige said.

"I guess Cullen didn't put the note in the book. So now what?" Drake asked.

Lin said, "We need to make sure we have this right, Paige. You let Logan have your science book. But first you made sure no papers were in the book."

"Yes. I made sure there weren't any papers in the book. Then I gave it to Logan," Paige said.

"So the note wasn't in the book when you gave it to Logan. And you're sure about that?" Drake asked.

"Yes. I made sure. I didn't want Logan to lose any of my notes."

"What did you do with the book, Logan?" Lin asked.

"What do you think I did with it? I took it to my science class," Logan said.

Lin said, "We know that, Logan. But what did you do with it after you got there? Did you let someone borrow it?"

"No. Why would I let someone borrow it? I needed it," Logan said.

Drake said, "This isn't helping Paige. I don't think we'll find out who wrote the note."

"Don't say that, Drake. We'll find out," Lin said.

"Yeah, Drake," Logan said.

"But how?" Drake asked.

Paige was wondering the same thing. Lunch was over. She didn't know who put the note in her book. And she didn't have any idea who could have done it.

Chapter 7

Later that day, Paige was in front of her apartment building. She was sitting on the steps. Paige was thinking about the note. And she still had no idea who wrote it.

Logan and Lin came over to the steps. They sat down.

"Has anyone called you, Paige?" Lin asked.

"What Lin really wants to know is this: Do you have a date to the dance yet?" Logan asked.

"That isn't what I asked," Lin said.

"I know. But that's what you really

want to know," Logan said.

Paige knew Logan was right. That was what Lin really wanted to know.

"No one asked me to the dance. I guess I'll stay home on Friday night. I won't go to the dance," Paige said.

"You can go without a date, Paige," Lin said.

"Yeah," Logan said.

Paige could go without a date. But Paige didn't plan on doing that.

"I won't go if I don't have a date," Paige said.

"Did you find out who wrote the note?" Lin asked.

"No," Paige said.

"Then we have to find out who did," Lin said.

"But how?" Paige asked.

"Yeah. How?" Logan asked.

"Someone must have put it in the book

when Logan had the book. So it must be someone in Logan's science class," Lin said.

"It had to be," Paige said.

"Someone who sits near you must have done it, Logan. Which guys sit near you in science class?" Lin asked.

Logan laughed.

"What's so funny?" Paige asked.

Paige didn't think Lin's question was that funny.

Logan said, "I just thought of something. And I think I know who your secret admirer is, Paige."

"Who?" both girls asked.

"Brett. He's always talking to you after class," Logan said.

Paige liked Brett. And she hoped he was her secret admirer. But she didn't think he was.

"You're wrong, Logan. Brett talks to me about English. But he doesn't talk to me about anything else," Paige said.

"Maybe. But he likes you. I'm sure he's your secret admirer," Logan said.

"Why do you think that?" Lin asked.

Paige wanted to know that, too.

Logan said, "I had to ask Mr. Zane something. And I had to go over to his desk to ask him. Brett sits next to my desk. He had time to put the note in the book then."

"You think he had time to do it when you were talking to Mr. Zane?" Lin asked.

"Yeah. And earlier Brett heard me tell Paige I needed to borrow her book. So he knew it was her book," Logan said.

Paige said, "I think you might be right, Logan. Brett might be my secret admirer. But how can I find out?"

"Ask him," Logan said.

"What do you want me to ask him? 'Are you my secret admirer, Brett?' I can't ask him that," Paige said.

"I'll ask him for you," Logan said.

"No," Paige said.

"Why?" Logan asked.

"What if he doesn't like me, Logan?" Paige asked.

"Then he would just say he doesn't like you," Logan said.

"Promise me you won't ask Brett," Paige said.

Logan didn't say anything.

"Promise me, Logan," Paige said.

Lin said, "Promise Paige, Logan."

"Okay. Okay," Logan said.

Paige didn't want Logan to ask Brett. But she needed to know soon. The dance was this Friday night.

Chapter 8

The next morning, Paige sat at the bus stop. Lin and Logan were there, too.

"Did Brett call you last night, Paige?" Lin asked.

"Yeah, Paige. Do you have a date yet?" Logan asked.

Paige knew why Lin asked her. Logan didn't have to tell her why.

"No. I don't have a date," Paige said.

Logan said, "Don't forget, Paige. I said I would ask Brett if he wrote the note. Do you want me to ask him?"

"No. I told you I didn't want you to

ask him. And you promised me that you wouldn't do that," Paige said.

"Yes, Logan. You did promise Paige," Lin said.

"Okay. I won't ask Brett. But let me know if you change your mind, Paige," Logan said.

"I won't change my mind, Logan," Paige said.

"Okay," Logan said.

Drake walked up to them. He said, "Did you find out for sure who wrote the note, Paige?"

"No," Paige said.

"Did anyone call and ask you to the dance?" Drake asked.

"No," Paige said. Paige wished people would stop asking her if she had a date to the school dance.

"Do you still want to go to the dance?" Drake asked. "I'll ask around, Paige. And

I'll find out who doesn't have a date. And I'll get a date for you."

Sometimes Drake could make Paige as mad as Logan did.

Paige said, "I can get my own date, Drake. I don't need you to get one for me. And, anyway, I don't want to go to the dance." But that wasn't true. Paige knew the other three didn't believe her either.

For a few minutes no one said anything.

But then Logan said, "I have an idea, Paige."

"What?" Drake asked.

"Yes, Logan. What?" Lin asked.

Paige hoped it wasn't about Logan finding a date for her.

Logan said, "I'm sure Brett likes Paige. And I'm sure he's her secret admirer. So I think Paige should tell Brett she got the note."

Paige said, "You can forget about that, Logan. I won't ask Brett if he's my secret admirer."

"I didn't say to do that, Paige. Just tell Brett you got the note. And you think someone in my science class put the note in your book. Ask him if he saw anyone put the note in there," Logan said.

"That sounds like a plan to me," Drake said.

Lin said, "You could do that, Paige. That isn't the same as asking Brett if he put the note there."

Drake said, "Yeah. And tell Brett you want to go to the school dance with that person."

"I'm not sure I should ask Brett about the note. But I'll think about it," Paige said.

"Good," Logan said.

But then Paige thought of something else.

"I just thought of something else," Paige said.

"What?" the other three asked at the same time.

"Maybe Brett has already asked someone to the dance," Paige said.

"I'll ask Brett in science if he has a date. Meet me outside of the class when class is over, Paige. And I'll tell you what I find out," Logan said.

Paige wanted to go to the dance. And she would like to go with Brett. So she didn't think anything was wrong with Logan's idea.

"Do you want me to do that, Paige?" Logan asked.

"Yes. But don't ask Brett about the note," Paige said.

The bus came. And they all got on the bus.

Paige wanted to know if Brett had a date. So she was in a hurry to get to school. And she was glad when the bus got there.

The morning went by slowly for Paige. But then it was time for Logan's science class to be over.

Paige hurried down the hall to Logan's classroom.

Logan walked out of the room. He came over to Paige.

Logan said, "Brett doesn't have a date. And he asked me if you did."

Paige was very glad to hear that.

Brett came out of the science class. And Logan hurried down the hall.

Brett came over to Paige. He said, "What did you do in English today?"

Paige told him. Then she said, "I need

your help, Brett. Can you help me with something?"

Brett seemed surprised. "Okay," he said.

"I let Logan borrow my science book. And someone put a note in it," she said.

Brett's face started to get red. So Paige was sure he had put the note in her book.

"Logan doesn't know who put the note in my book. And I hope you saw who put it there. The person wants to go to the dance with me. And I want to go with him, too. But I don't know who he is," Paige said.

"You really would like to go with him?" Brett asked.

"Yes. But I don't know who he is," Paige said.

But now Paige did know who he was. She knew he was Brett.

Brett smiled. Then he said, "I wrote the note, Paige. And I want to take you to the dance. Will you go with me?"

"Yes," Paige said. She smiled.

Now Paige had a date to the dance. And she was glad her secret admirer wasn't a secret any longer.